For PETE, TATER TOT & JER JER

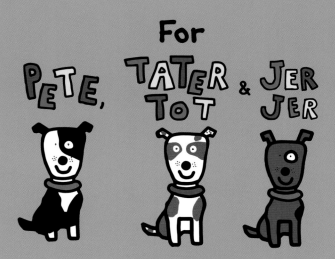

Also by Todd Parr

A complete list of Todd's books and more information can be found at toddparr.com.

About This Book

The illustrations for this book were created on a drawing tablet using an iMac, starting with bold black lines and dropping in color with Adobe Photoshop. This book was edited by Megan Tingley and Anna Prendella and designed by Lynn El-Roeiy. The production was supervised by Bernadette Flinn, and the production editor was Marisa Finkelstein. The text was set in Todd Parr's signature font.

Little, Brown and Company • Hachette Book Group • 1290 Avenue of the Americas, New York, NY 10104 • Visit us at LBYR.com • First Edition: April 2020 • Little, Brown and Company is a division of Hachette Book Group, Inc. • The Little, Brown name and logo are trademarks of Hachette Book Group, Inc. • The publisher is not responsible for websites (or their content) that are not owned by the publisher. • Library of Congress Cataloging-in-Publication Data • Parr, Todd, author, illustrator. • Title: The birthday book / Todd Parr. • Description: First edition. | New York: Megan Tingley Books/Little, Brown and Company, 2020. | Audience: Ages 3–6 | Summary: Illustrations and simple text reveal the fun things you can do on your birthday. • Identifiers: LCCN 2019031298 | ISBN 9780316506632 (hardcover) • Subjects: CYAC: Birthdays—Fiction. • Classification: LCC PZ7.P2447 Bi 2020 | DDC [E]—dc23 | LC record available at https://lccn.loc.gov/2019031298 • ISBNs: 978-0-316-50663-2 (hardcover) • PRINTED IN CHINA • APS • 10 9 8 7 6 5 4 3 2 1

THE BIRTHDAY BOOK

TODD PARR

Megan Tingley Books

LITTLE, BROWN AND COMPANY

NEW YORK BOSTON

You might be one year old.

Or you might be one hundred years old.

Today is the day to celebrate YOU!

Happy birthday!

You can eat breakfast in bed.

Or eat macaroni and cheese in the bathtub.

You can get dressed up.

Or just wear your birthday suit.

You can celebrate with family and friends.

Or all by yourself.

You can eat cake.

And make a wish.

You might get presents.

You might get hugs.

HAPPY TO

Today is a day for a birthday party.

Do something special or new.

Party like an animal.

Or curl up with someone you love.

It's a day to be happy and think about all

HAPPY

the things you can do now that you're older.

Tomorrow you start a new year, and it won't be long until another birthday is here. Don't forget to celebrate every day. The End. ♡ Love, Todd

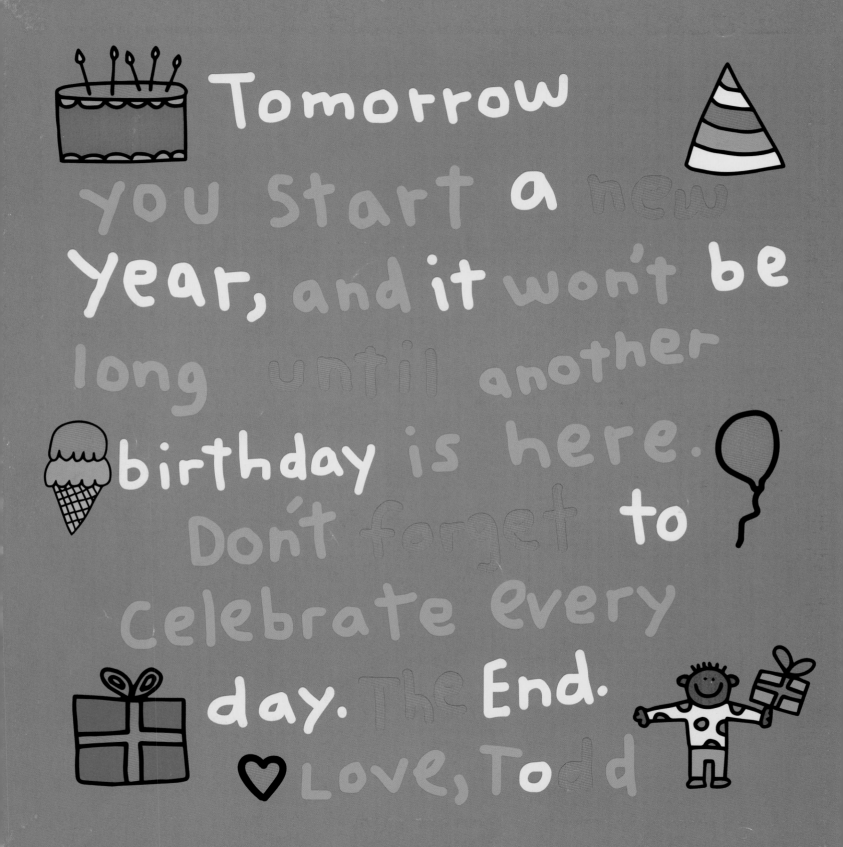